Basil and Hillary

JANE BRESKIN ZALBEN

MACMILLAN PUBLISHING CO., INC.
New York
COLLIER MACMILLAN PUBLISHERS
London

10 9 8 7 6 5 4 3 2 1

Library of Congress Cataloging in Publication Data
Zalben, Jane Breskin. Basil and Hillary.
[1. Domestic animals—Fiction.   2. Farm life—Fiction]
I. Title.   PZ7.Z254Bas   [E]   74–19043
ISBN 0–02–793720–8

The four-color illustrations were prepared as black pen
and ink drawings, with overlays for red, blue and yel-
low. The typeface is Alphatype Century Text, with
display set in Cooper Black.

To Mom and Dad
who made my dreams possible

Basil and Hillary fell in love
and decided to build a house.

They had many neighbors
who wanted to help.

Ellie the cat meowed,
"I'll scratch out a path."

Gretchen the cow mooed,
"I'll cut the grass."

Humphrey the donkey brayed,
"I'll scoop a pond."

Oliver the dog barked,
"I'll dig a well."

Henrietta the lamb baaed,
"I'll make the blankets."

Harry the goat bleated,
"I'll nail the fence."

Justin the rooster crowed,
"I'll be the weathervane."

Simpson the horse whinnied,
"I'll hoe a vegetable patch."

Ginger the hen clucked,
"I'll plant the seeds."

Beatrice the rabbit sniffed.
"I'll eat them!"

Sam the mule just snoozed.

Suddenly it began to rain.

The pond overflowed.

The grass drowned.

The path disappeared.

The blankets unraveled.

The seeds washed away.

The vegetable patch turned to mud.

Justin went round in circles.

And Sam still slept.

The others ran under a peach tree,

where they ate peaches and told
stories until the rain stopped.

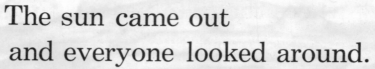

The sun came out
and everyone looked around.

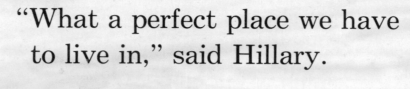

"What a perfect place we have
to live in," said Hillary.

And all their friends agreed.